THE LAST QUEST OF GILGAMESH

RETOLD AND ILLUSTRATED BY LUDMILA ZEMAN

TUNDRA BOOKS

AT THE MOUTH OF A RIVER at the end of the earth a man lies, near death.
Could this be Gilgamesh, the all-powerful King of Uruk,
loved by his people, famous throughout the ancient world
for the magnificent wall he had built around his city?
What has brought him to this desperate state in this lonely place?

It was the fear of Death. Death had taken his dearest friend, Enkidu.
Earlier it had taken the beautiful Shamhat whom they both loved.
As Gilgamesh watched their spirits fly off as birds,
he resolved to get rid of Death before it took him from his people.
His last quest would be to find the secret of immortality.

He had searched far and found nothing. Now as he lay exhausted,
he heard a familiar voice and opened his eyes to see a bird.

T HE SPIRIT OF SHAMHAT had returned to help him. "Don't give up, Gilgamesh," she urged. "Look! There! Between those peaks of Mashu Mountain, the Sun God goes down to sleep. By day he sees everything. He knows where immortality lies. Rise up and follow his path." Gilgamesh called on strength he did not know he had and got up to continue his search.

THE MOUNTAIN WAS STEEP and he could not keep up. The Sun went down and darkness fell.
The moon cast eerie shadows. Jagged stones tore at his clothes and beasts attacked him.
He fought them off and pressed on, determined to catch up with the Sun.
As he came near the top of the mountain, he heard a small, desperate cry for help.

A LION CUB had fallen off the cliff. Gilgamesh reached down and rescued the little animal as Enkidu had once saved him from falling off the city wall. Two giant scorpions screamed: "How dare you come here! We guard the Kingdom of the Sun. Go back if you want to live." Gilgamesh faced them defiantly. "I have come to find the Sun God. Let us pass," he ordered.

THE SCORPIONS were amazed at the courage of Gilgamesh. "We will help you and your little friend."
They lowered Gilgamesh and the lion cub into a deep abyss. "Find the light and follow it."
Gilgamesh was in a freezing tunnel of terrifying creatures. He hugged the frightened cub close.
After long hours of wandering in the dark, he finally saw a ray of light ahead and moved toward it.

GILGAMESH CAME OUT into brilliant sunshine. It was the garden of the Sun God. It was paradise. Never did leaves sparkle so like jewels, flowers give off such perfumes, animals appear so gentle. "Why not rest here?" the Sun God offered. But Gilgamesh refused. "I must find immortality. Help me." "The only human who knows that secret is Utnapishtim," the Sun God said. "I will lead you to him."

GILGAMESH FOLLOWED THE SUN as it led him across the burning sands of the desert.
The lion cub collapsed from the heat. Gilgamesh lifted him gently onto his back and kept going.
Half-blinded by the dust, longing for a drink of water, he struggled on, dragging his feet in the sand.
At last, on the distant horizon, he saw a magnificent house covered with vines.

HE REACHED IT, exhausted. At the door a beautiful woman looked with horror at the ragged stranger. "I am no beggar," Gilgamesh said. "I am a king. I have come to find Utnapishtim and immortality." "You can't reach him," the woman said. "He lives on an island protected by the Waters of Death. Give up the search. Stay with me. I am Siduri. I make wine for the Gods. Drink, dance and be happy."

"I HAVE COME through too much to give up now," Gilgamesh said. "Help me. Lend me your boat."
"Only the Sun can cross those deadly waters," Siduri warned. "They destroy every oar they touch."
Determined, Gilgamesh went into the forest. There, he chopped a hundred and twenty poles and set out.
He reached the deadly part of the sea. Pole after pole was swallowed, leaving only stumps in his hands.

THE WATERS raged wildly. Gilgamesh pushed on, throwing away each stump and grabbing a new pole. Around him floated the bones of creatures that had been devoured by the Waters of Death.

THE SKIES darkened and a fierce wind blew up as his last pole was eaten away. He could see the island. But how could he reach it? "I must not fail now," he cried. "I am too close to the end of my search."

IN A LAST desperate attempt, he took off his torn shirt and raised it to the wind to make a sail. Utnapishtim watched, amazed as the boat reached shore. "Who are you to come here — god or man?"
"I am Gilgamesh, King of Uruk," came the proud reply. "I come to ask the secret of immortality."
"Do not seek what you cannot have," Utnapishtim replied. "Only gods can live forever."

"BUT YOU WERE ONCE no different than me," Gilgamesh argued. "How did you become immortal?"
"To know that," Utnapishtim answered, "you must stay awake six days and seven nights.
My story is carved into this wall. You may not sleep while I read it." The test sounded easy.
Gilgamesh promised and Utnapishtim began. "When I was king of Shuruppak, the people became evil."

"THE GODS decided to destroy the earth with a great flood. Because I was a good man, I was warned. I was told to build a great ark and to gather into it my family and each kind of animal and plant. As soon as I finished, the storm came. For six days and seven nights, it rained, and the earth was flooded.

"ONLY MY BOAT survived. When the rain stopped and the water subsided, it came to rest on a mountain. I fell to my knees in gratitude. I let out the animals and set out the plants to start life anew. In that moment the gods descended in a great light and bestowed immortality upon me and my wife."

UTNAPISHTIM finished his story and he looked down. Gilgamesh was asleep. He had failed the test. Utnapishtim spoke with sadness: "Gilgamesh, a mortal you came here. A mortal you must leave." Gilgamesh begged. "Give me another chance!" Utnapishtim took mercy on him and weakened. "See that light far in the sea? A plant grows there that grants youth to all who eat it. It will not keep you from dying, but it will keep you young as long as you live."

GILGAMESH sailed out again across the deadly sea. He reached the glowing spot and leapt into the water, not knowing if it would destroy him. He grasped the plant and struggled with it to the surface. Triumphantly, he showed it to the little lion: "This will make the old people of Uruk young again. When I am old, I, too, shall eat it and get back my lost youth and strength."

Gilgamesh set out on the long voyage home. He had not found immortality, but he held a treasure.

THE BOAT PASSED a lovely island and Gilgamesh stopped to eat fresh fruit and take some rest.
He fell into a peaceful sleep, dreaming of the happiness he was bringing back to his people.
He did not see the serpent slithering down from a tree. He awoke to hear the evil voice of Ishtar.
"I have my revenge," she screamed. "You have nothing." She had swallowed the flower while he slept.

ISHTAR NOW HAD the revenge she wanted ever since Gilgamesh rejected her offer of marriage.
"Ishtar, you wicked one," Gilgamesh cried. "You killed my friend Enkidu. Now you have killed hope."
He hugged the little lion and wept. He had come through so much to have it all end like this.
Suddenly, he heard a voice calling to him. His beloved Enkidu had returned. They embraced with joy.

"SHAMHAT SENT ME from the underworld to help you," Enkidu explained.
"Sit on my back with your little lion. I have something to show you."
Together they flew over the rivers of Sumer as far as the city of Uruk.
Gilgamesh saw his kingdom from above for the first time,
its great temples, its fine houses, its beautiful gardens and,
most impressive, the majestic wall he had built around it all.
His heart filled with a pride and happiness greater than he had ever known.

"Here, Gilgamesh, is the immortality you have sought," Enkidu said.
"The city you built, the courage you showed, the good you have done.
You will live in the hearts of people forever."

The epic of Gilgamesh is one of the oldest stories in the world; it was inscribed onto clay tablets over 5000 years ago in Mesopotamia (where Iraq and Syria are today). The different peoples of the area told many versions of the story, but in all of them, Gilgamesh, the king of the city of Uruk, goes out in search of everlasting life after the death of his friend Enkidu. That his search ends in failure, because only gods are immortal, makes Gilgamesh the first tragic (as well as human) hero in world literature.

Because many of the world's earliest civilizations built their first cities along rivers, stories of floods are almost universal. Mesopotamia means "the land between the rivers," and the flood story told by Utnapishtim (known in Judeo-Christian tradition as Noah) was an important "wisdom" inserted into the epic of Gilgamesh in all its versions. On a map, one can see two rivers in Iraq: the Tigris and Euphrates. The rivers would flood unpredictably, bringing disaster to the people in the cities built along the riverbanks and influencing the way they viewed the world. When the rivers changed course, Gilgamesh's beloved city of Uruk was abandoned and the land surrounding it became the desert it is today.

The Mesopotamians were the first to describe a terrible place called hell. It would come to be accepted in Judeo-Christian beliefs. The terrors that Gilgamesh passes through on his quest reemerged in classical literature and in medieval art. The 19th-century artist Gustave Doré was inspired by these images to illustrate Dante's *Divine Comedy*. Ludmila Zeman has borrowed back from Doré, but her most important contribution has been the research into the statuary and relics preserved in the world's leading museums and her imaginative use of these to re-create the ancient world.

For example, on tablets found across Mesopotamia, Gilgamesh is shown accompanied by lions to symbolize his strength and courage. Zeman has a lion cub accompany the king on his quest.

The immortality of Gilgamesh was assured by something much larger than his famous city. He is the first hero of Western literature, embodying all the virtues we associate with heroes: courage, compassion, loyalty, tenacity in hardship and dedication to a vision. From Ulysses of ancient Greece and Aeneas of Rome, from King Arthur of Britain down to the interplanetary travelers of today's popular culture, all our heroes owe their appeal to the standards of legendary heroism set by Gilgamesh. He is indeed immortal.

I would like to dedicate this book to all the archeologists who resurrected the beautiful but almost forgotten ancient epic of Gilgamesh.   — *Ludmila Zeman*

Copyright © 1995 by Ludmila Zeman

Published in Canada by Tundra Books, *McClelland & Stewart Young Readers*, 481 University Avenue, Toronto, Ontario M5G 2E9

Published in the United States by Tundra Books of Northern New York, P.O. Box 1030, Plattsburgh, New York 12901

Library of Congress Catalog Number: 93-61787

All rights reserved. The use of any part of this publication reproduced, transmitted in any form or by any means, electronic, mechanical, photocopying, recording, or otherwise, or stored in a retrieval system, without the prior written consent of the publisher - or, in case of photocopying or other reprographic copying, a licence from the Canadian Copyright Licensing Agency - is an infringement of the copyright law.

Canadian Cataloguing in Publication Data

Zeman, Ludmila
   The last quest of Gilgamesh
ISBN 0-88776-328-6 (bound)   ISBN 0-88776-380-4 (pbk.)
I. Title.
PS8599.E492L38   jC813'.54   C96-930977-5
PZ7.Z45La

We acknowledge the support of the Canada Council for the Arts for our publishing program.

The artist acknowledges the generous support of the Ministry of Culture of the Government of Quebec in the creation of the artwork for this book.

Design by Dan O'Leary

Printed in Hong Kong by South China Printing Co. Ltd.

2 3 4 5 6   01 00 99 98 97   2 3 4 5 6   02 01 00 99 98